Ms Wiz

RULES OK!

PRAISE FOR THE MS WIZ BOOKS:

"Funny, magical . . . with wicked pictures
by Tony Ross, it's the closest thing you'll
get to Roald Dahl"
The Times

"Wonderfully funny and exciting"
Books for Keeps

"Ms Wiz is everyone's favourite"
Young Calibre Library

"Hilarious and hysterical"
Sunday Times

"The fantastic Ms Wiz books"
Malorie Blackman

Other Ms Wiz books

TERENCE BLACKER

Ms Wiz
RULES OK!

Illustrated by
TONY ROSS

ANDERSEN PRESS
LONDON

First published in Great Britain in 2010
by Andersen Press Limited
20 Vauxhall Bridge Road
London SW1V 2SA
www.andersenpress.co.uk

2 3 4 5 6 7 8 9 10

Power-crazy Ms Wiz first published in 1992 by Piccadilly Press Limited
Ms Wiz Goes Live first published in 1990 by Piccadilly Press Limited

British Library Cataloguing in Publication Data available.

ISBN 978 184 270 858 3

Printed and bound in Great Britain by Clays Ltd, Elcograf S.p.A.

Ms Wiz

GOES LIVE

CHAPTER ONE
PARENT PROBLEMS

It was an evening like any other at the Smith household.

Mr Smith was in the living room reading a newspaper and drinking a can of beer. Mrs Smith was shouting at him from the kitchen. Caroline, their eldest child, was trying to do her homework and wondering what it was about parents that made them argue all the time. And her three-year-old sister, known to everyone as Little Musha, was in front of the television, carefully working some chocolate cake into the carpet.

There was a crash of cutlery from the kitchen.

"I work all day!" Mrs Smith said loudly. "And have you done the

washing-up when I come home, or
cooked the children's supper, or done
the hoovering or made the beds?
Have you heck!"

"Yak yak yak," said Mr Smith,
taking a swig of beer. "I've been out
looking for a job. I'm tired."

Caroline sighed and took the
remains of the chocolate cake from
her little sister, who started crying.

There was another crash of plates
from the kitchen. "All I can say,"
muttered Mrs Smith, "is that you've
changed. You're not the man I
married."

"That's true," said Mr Smith. "I was
happy then."

"Happy!" Mrs Smith gave an angry
laugh. "You've always been a
miserable useless, lazy—"

"Mum," said Caroline, who knew
exactly when to interrupt her parents'
rows. "I'm trying to do my homework

and Musha keeps trying to turn the television on."

"It's my favourite programme," said Musha.

"What is?" asked Caroline.

Musha thought for a moment. "Whatever's on now," she said.

"*Please* tell her, Mum—"

"STOP FIGHTING!" Their mother stamped her foot. A plate fell to the ground and smashed. There was silence for a moment. Mrs Smith sighed. "Let her watch television, Caro," she said. "At least, we get some peace that way."

"What about my homework?"

Mr Smith wandered into the kitchen. "I'm going to the pub," he mumbled.

"The *pub*?" gasped Mrs Smith.

"Why don't you both go out?" said Caroline, quickly joining them.

"Great idea," said her mother

tearfully. "We could go and watch a terrible film and grumble about it afterwards or eat at a restaurant and realise we have nothing to say to one another, or just watch other people having fun in a pub."

Mr Smith put his arm around his wife's shoulders. "Come on, love," he said. "Let's have an evening out. We both need a break."

"And what about a babysitter?" asked Mrs Smith.

Just then the doorbell rang. Caroline opened the door.

"Good evening," said a young woman with a clipboard under her arm. "I'm doing a survey for—"

"Ms Wiz!" Caroline smiled. "What on earth are you doing here?"

"I'm doing a survey for—"

"Hey, Mum, Dad," Caroline shouted over her shoulder. "This is Ms Wiz, who did all the magic things

at school and visited Jack in hospital and found Lizzie's stolen cat and saved the library by bringing Peter Rabbit and Frankenstein to life."

"Not that witch woman?" said Mr Smith suspiciously.

"Paranormal Operative actually," said Ms Wiz. "It's not quite the same."

"Can Paranormal Operatives babysit?" asked Mrs Smith.

"Well," said Ms Wiz. "I'm really here to complete this survey."

"What's it about, Ms Wiz?" asked Caroline. "Something magic?"

Ms Wiz looked at the clipboard and took a deep breath. "I need to know how many windows people have in their houses, how big the windows are, if they're happy with their windows and, if not, how they would like them changed, whether their windows go up and down or open sideways or slide, if they're draughty when the wind blows, whether they're made of wood or metal, how often the window cleaner comes, how much he charges, how many windows *he* has at home, does he wash them with a sponge or a cloth or bits of newspaper and does he whistle while he works and—"

"Boring," said Little Musha.

"I suppose it is rather," said Ms Wiz. "All right. I'll babysit for you." She stepped into the house.

"Are you reliable?" asked Mrs Smith.

"Reliable?" Caroline laughed. "She was a teacher. You can't be more reliable than that, can you?"

"Mmm," said Mr Smith uncertainly. "Wasn't there something about her keeping a rat up her sleeve?"

"That was just a rumour," said Caroline, handing her father his coat

and holding the front door open for
him. "You both go out and enjoy
yourselves."

Mumbling, Mr and Mrs Smith made
their way out of the house. As Ms
Wiz, Caroline and Little Musha waved
them goodbye, they were arguing as
to how they should spend the evening.

"Phew!" said Ms Wiz, closing the
front door. She pulled a rat out of her

sleeve. "Can Herbert have a run now?"

"Survey, eh?" said Caroline with a smile. "You knew I needed help."

Ms Wiz shrugged. "I go where magic's needed," she said. "So what's the problem here?"

Caroline frowned. "I always seem to be sorting things out. Musha, Mummy, Daddy. I'm only nine but I never have any fun these days."

"We'll see about that," said Ms Wiz.

Herbert, the magic rat, was scurrying towards the kitchen when Little Musha picked him up rather roughly.

"Don't like rats," she said, nose to nose with Herbert.

Ms Wiz smiled. "Not even rats with miniature water-pistols in their right ears?"

"What?" said Little Musha.

At that moment a jet of water

squirted from Herbert's right ear,
hitting Little Musha in the eye.
"Ow!" she shouted, dropping the rat
and starting to cry.

When Little Musha cried, the
glasses in the kitchen rattled, the
neighbours shut their windows and
cats disappeared up trees in terror
at the noise. It was like a police
siren.

"This is Little Musha," Caroline

shouted to Ms Wiz. "She's—"
Caroline remembered a phrase that
grown-ups liked to use when
discussing her sister "—she's quite a
character."

"Little Musha, eh?" said Ms Wiz.
"Is that a nice Indian name?"

Little Musha stopped crying. "I'm
called Musha," she said, treading on
Ms Wiz's toe, "because I mush
people."

"Her real name's Annie," Caroline
explained. "But she's going through
a mushing phase and likes to be called
Little Musha."

"Well, she had better not mush
me," said Ms Wiz firmly. "And what
are we going to do tonight, Little
Musha?"

"Television."

"Oh no," said Caroline. "We could
do amazing things now that Ms Wiz
is here. She can turn people into

animals, make things disappear. She can fly."

Musha thought for a moment. "Television," she said.

"See?" said Caroline. "No fun."

"What's wrong with television?" asked Ms Wiz.

"But we always watch—"

Ms Wiz held up her hand and smiled. "Trust me," she said.

CHAPTER TWO
JIMMY GOES BANANAS

"You're getting *smaller*, Ms Wiz!"

Caroline and Ms Wiz were watching the What-a-Load-of-Show-Offs Show on television when Little Musha began to stare at Ms Wiz.

"It's true," she said. "You really are getting smaller, Ms Wiz."

"Yes," said Ms Wiz. "I'm thinking of going into television."

"Oh no," said Caroline, who now saw that her sister was right and that Ms Wiz was shrinking rapidly. "Don't go all small on us. You're meant to be babysitting."

Ms Wiz was now slightly smaller than Little Musha. "You can shrink too, if you like," she said.

"But then what happens?" asked Caroline.

"We enjoy some television, from inside the television set."

"Yeah!" said Little Musha. "Do it, Ms Wiz."

When Ms Wiz was around, the strangest things seemed normal. Within seconds, Caroline discovered that the furniture in her living room appeared to have grown to an enormous size. A fly on a wall nearby looked as big as a jumbo jet.

"Follow me," said Ms Wiz to Caroline and Little Musha. They all climbed on to a nearby matchstick.

"Hold tight," shouted Ms Wiz as the sound of a low hum filled the room. The matchstick hovered above the ground and then carried the three of them on to the television set.

"What about Herbert?" asked Caroline.

"It's all right," said Ms Wiz.
"He's in my pocket – as tiny as
we are."

"I hate Herbert," muttered Little
Musha, remembering the water
pistol. "I hope he disappears
altogether."

"Now how exactly are we going to
get into this set?" Ms Wiz was
tapping the top of the television.
"Here we are," she said, opening a

small trapdoor. Some steps led into the dark inside.

Little Musha gasped. "Ms Wiz is going into the telly," she said. "What are we going to do now?"

Caroline remembered that she was meant to be the responsible one. "But we're not even allowed to touch the back of the television because it's so dangerous," she shouted down the steps. "I don't think Mum and Dad would like it if we got right inside."

"Don't worry," Ms Wiz's voice echoed in the darkness. "This is magic TV."

"Come on then," said Little Musha.

Caroline sighed, took her little sister's hand and stepped into the television set.

"Ready?" said Ms Wiz, when they reached the bottom of the steps. In front of them was a large door with a notice saying "STUDIO 5 – DO NOT

ENTER WHEN THE RED LIGHT IS
ON". The red light above the door
shone brightly.

"What's the light for?" asked
Caroline.

"It means they're making a
programme," said Ms Wiz. "It's
probably the one we were watching.
Let's go in and see."

She opened the door and all three
of them were dazzled by bright
lights.

"And now," a voice was saying,
"the What-a-Load-of-Show-Offs Show
welcomes our next contestant."

As her eyes grew accustomed to the
studio lights, Caroline saw a man
with a yellow jersey walking towards
them.

"It's Jimmy," she whispered. "He's
the star of What-a-Load-of-Show-Offs."

"Yes," said Ms Wiz. "And we're on
his show."

"I want to go home," said Little Musha.

Jimmy took her hand and held it tightly. "Hello, little girl," he said, putting his face close to Little Musha's. "And what's our name then?"

"Musha."

"Musha." Jimmy winked at the camera which had followed him across the studio. "What a lovely name. Why do they call you that?"

"Careful," Caroline murmured, but it was too late.

"Because I like mushing." Little Musha reached out for Jimmy's nose and twisted it hard.

"Aaaaagghh!" The star of What-a-Load-of-Show-Offs hopped from one foot to the other until Little Musha let go of his nose. "Aaaaggghhh . . . ha . . . ha . . . ha . . . Isn't live television great, folks?"

"Why have you got tears in your eyes?" asked Little Musha.

"I'll tell you after the show," said Jimmy through clenched teeth. "Come over here and play our lovely quiz game."

Ms Wiz and Caroline took a seat at the back of the studio as Little Musha reluctantly allowed herself to be led to a big chair.

"Now every time I say a word,"

said Jimmy. "You have to say another word that's a bit like it. So I say 'rain' and you say 'cloud' or 'sun' or 'wet'. All right?"

Little Musha nodded. Her chin was set like a boxer's before a fight. This was never a good sign.

Jimmy smiled. "Now—"

"Then," said Little Musha.

"I haven't started yet, *silly*."

"Billy," said Little Musha.

"No—"

"Yes."

"Very funny," said Jimmy, whose face was now a bright red colour. "The first word is . . . hair."

"Pull."

"Ice cream."

"Carpet."

"Bedtime."

"Scream."

"Toe."

"Stamp."

"Stamp?" said Jimmy. "That's not right, is it? Now where's the connection between toe and—"

Little Musha brought her sharp little heel down hard on Jimmy's toe.

"EEEERRRRGGGGHHHH!" Jimmy staggered back. "Where's a doctor? Where's my agent? Get this child out of here! I never wanted to work with children anyway. I was going to be an actor."

"I think we've outstayed our welcome," said Ms Wiz quietly to Caroline. "Get your sister and follow me."

"Someone take this little brute away," Jimmy was shouting.

Caroline hurried forward and grabbed Musha.

"That was fun," said Little Musha.

"Maybe for you," said Caroline, dragging her out of the studio. "For me, it's home from home. Now come *on*."

Ms Wiz was waiting for them at a door marked "EXIT".

"Don't like Jimmy," said Little Musha as they hurried out of the studio.

Ms Wiz sighed. "I don't think he's wild about you either," she said.

CHAPTER THREE
"NO AUTOGRAPHS, PERLEASE!"

"No, of course you're not a little brute," said Caroline, holding Musha's hand as they hurried along a brightly-lit corridor. "Is she, Ms Wiz?"

"Certainly not," said Ms Wiz.

"Where are we going to now?" asked Little Musha.

"Let's try and find a programme with a bit less violence," said Ms Wiz. "If we go on like this, we could get banned from the television."

Caroline had an idea. "Maybe I could—"

"Hey," shouted Little Musha as they turned a corner. "Cartoons!"

"Oh, forget it," sighed Caroline.

Ahead of them, standing outside a

studio door, sipping tea, were two cartoon characters, a cat and a mouse.

Little Musha gasped. "It's Tom and Jerry," she said.

Jerry, the cartoon mouse, gave a weary smile. "No autographs, perlease," he said. "Not when we're resting between takes."

"I thought that Tom and you were meant to be enemies," said Caroline. "On television, you're always chasing each other about and hitting one another over the head."

"Don't believe everything you see on the screen," said Jerry. "We're enemies when the cameras roll but in real life, we're buddies."

"Real life!" Caroline smiled. "But you're cartoon characters."

"Hey, lady," said Jerry, putting on his well-known frown. "Don't knock cartoons, perlease. Like this evening, we're rehearsing a scene where Tom's

playing golf. He rolls me up into a
little ball and wallops me three
hundred yards. I bounce off a tree,
rebound off a passing seagull, catch
Tom in the stomach and flatten him
against a wall, which then collapses
on top of him."

"You *rehearse* that?" asked Caroline.

"How else d'you think we get it
right?" said Tom. "Magic?"

"The producer says we could use
stand-ins but we like to do our own
stunts," said Jerry. "Talking of which,
it's time for me to run Tom over with
a steamroller."

Tom winked. "Showbiz!" he said.
"Don't you just love it?"

"Can I come?" asked Little Musha.

"No," said Ms Wiz and Caroline
at the same time. Musha took a
deep breath, sniffed a couple of
times and burst into tears at
maximum volume.

A woman hurried down the corridor towards them.

"*Ssshhh!*" she went. "How can we make television programmes with that terrible din? We've already had a disaster tonight with Jimmy throwing a tantrum on the What-a-Load-of-Show-Offs Show."

"Oh dear," said Ms Wiz, trying to keep a straight face. "We wouldn't know about that. We're just here on a visit."

"And what exactly are you here to see?" asked the woman.

Caroline put up a hand. "I was hoping—"

"We're looking for a really nice show," Ms Wiz interrupted.

"Nice?" The woman scratched her head. "There's not much demand for that these days. I suppose you could try our new series, Wild, Woolly and Weally Intewesting. They're doing a programme on extinct species at the moment, downstairs in Studio 9B."

The red light outside Studio 9B was shining brightly and there was a sign on the door which said, "QUIET! EXTINCT ANIMALS – DO NOT DISTURB!"

"What does extinct mean?" asked Little Musha.

"It means that they're the type of animals that no longer exist in the world," said Caroline.

"How can they be disturbed then?"

"I think it's a sort of television joke," said Ms Wiz, gently pushing the studio door open.

"Wow!" said Caroline.

Studio 9B had been decorated like a jungle, full of trees and creepers and the sound of exotic birds. In the centre of the studio, a big man with a beard was talking breathlessly in front of a camera.

"And so," he said. "Over litewally hundweds of centuwies, species changed, evolved and adapted to the world's enviwonment. If they haven't changed, many of them have pewished, died out, become extinct. Like—" the man walked across the studio to where a model of a strange-looking animal stood "—like Tywannosauwus Wex."

"Why aren't the animals moving?" whispered Little Musha.

"Because they're extinct," said Caroline.

A faint humming noise was coming from Ms Wiz. "I wonder if this programme needs livening up," she said.

"And then," the bearded man continued, "there's the dodo, a bird that died out almost two hundwed years ago." He walked to where Ms

Wiz stood. "Here we have a stuffed model of the dodo – as you can see, it's vewy vewy dead and extinct."

At that moment, the dodo put its head on one side and pecked at something on the studio floor.

"Now that's weally wather stwange," said the bearded man nervously. "Extinct animals don't usually move like that."

The dodo flapped its wings and flew on to a branch. "*Vewy* odd,' said the television presenter, scratching his beard. "The dodo can't fly. Or couldn't fly. I think I must be dweaming."

"Off you go, Herbert," muttered Ms Wiz, releasing the magic rat from her sleeve. Herbert stood on her arm, then spread his front legs and started to fly, like a small bird. After circling around Ms Wiz a couple of times, he flew across the studio.

The bearded man was climbing the tree towards the dodo when he noticed Herbert, hovering delicately a few inches away from his nose.

"Good gwacious me!" he said with a hint of panic in his voice. "This looks vewy like a type of humming-bird, except it's a wat – it's a sort of humming-wat." He sat down heavily on a branch. "I must be ill. I'm seeing things," he said. "Turn the wuddy camewas off."

"Cut!" The loud shout came from a man in shirtsleeves who was now hurrying across the studio.

"What on earth's going on?" he asked.

"The dodo was alive," said the bearded man weakly. "Then I was buzzed by a humming-wat."

"The dodo?' The man in shirtsleeves looked up at the tree, where now the stuffed dodo was standing lifelessly. "Who put it up there?"

"It flew," moaned the bearded man. "And then I saw a humming-wat."

"Come on," said Ms Wiz, quietly putting Herbert up her sleeve. "I think it's time for us all to leave the jungle."

"So why don't you magic lots of extinct animals back to life?" Caroline asked after they had crept out of Studio 9B. "I'd love to see a real live dinosaur."

"My spells don't last that long," said Ms Wiz. "A few minutes at the mo—"

"Excuse me," said a woman, hurrying down the corridor towards them. "Are you the replacement newsreader?"

"Newsreader?" said Ms Wiz. "Ah, yes. That's me."

"Andrew, our normal reader, has a terrible cold and has completely lost his voice," said the woman. "You're on the air in five minutes so you had all better follow me."

"News?" said Caroline. "I thought we were here for fun."

"We are," said Ms Wiz. "I think this could be tremendous fun."

"But what about—?"

"Right," said Ms Wiz, turning to the woman. "Where's my studio?" she said.

CHAPTER FOUR
GOOD NEWS FOR
REALLY NICE PEOPLE

"It's coming up to ten o'clock and, in a few seconds' time, we'll be going over to the newsroom for the news, read by Dolores Wisdom."

Caroline and Little Musha sat in a small room next door to where Ms Wiz was about to read the news and watched her through a big window between the two rooms. Beside them sat the producer, who was looking very nervous.

"She has done this before, hasn't she?" he asked Caroline.

"Probably," said Caroline.

"Because once she's started, we can't interrupt her, you know," warned the producer. "This is going out live."

"I'm sure she'll make it really . . . entertaining," said Caroline.

"Entertaining?" The producer looked more worried than ever. "I just want her to read the words on the little screen in front of her." He looked at a clock on the wall.

"Cue, Miss Wisdom," he said, holding his hand up.

"Good evening," said Ms Wiz, wearing her most serious expression

and reading the words in front of her.
"It's ten o'clock and here are the
news headlines. There has been a
plane crash in Italy. The economy is
looking worse than ever. The
government says it's everyone else's
fault. More wind and rain are forecast
throughout the country. A famous
actor has died. And—" Ms Wiz
hesitated for a moment and said,
"This is all a bit depressing, isn't it?"

"Hang on," said the producer next door. "Depressing? That wasn't in the script."

"You can hear all the gloomy news somewhere else," said Ms Wiz with a smile. "In the meantime, here's the good news for really nice people. Mr and Mrs Smith of 91 Elmtree Road went out tonight and had a very enjoyable time—"

"Whaaaaat?" said the producer. "Has she gone mad?"

"This," continued Ms Wiz, "after a grim start to the evening, during which Mrs Smith called Mr Smith miserable and lazy and then broke a plate—"

"How did she know that?" asked Little Musha.

"Listening at the door, probably," said Caroline.

"—but all has ended well, with the Smiths enjoying some fish and chips, just like the old days, followed by a romantic walk in the park. Their children, Caroline and Musha, have been shrunk by the babysitter."

The producer was now standing in front of the window and waving wildly at Ms Wiz, who waved back before going on with the news.

"Rats are getting nicer, it was officially announced tonight. And we have a rat spokesperson with us in the studio." Ms Wiz pulled Herbert the rat out of her sleeve. "So, Mr Herbert," she said. "Why have you rats suddenly decided to clean up your act?"

"Basically," said Herbert, looking towards the camera, "we're tired of the bad publicity. People say we're unfriendly, dirty and spread diseases and frankly, at the end of the day, this is not what we're about."

"And so what will you be doing about it?"

"First of all, we'll be cleaning our teeth," said Herbert. "There's no doubt that bright yellow teeth in a rat gives a very bad first impression. Then we'll be taking baths every day, and generally coming out of the closet and joining family life, rolling playfully around on the carpet, playing with the kids and so on."

"What about cats?" asked Ms Wiz.

"That's still a bit of a grey area," said Herbert. "But we hope to negotiate a peace settlement with them very soon."

"Thank you, Mr Herbert," said Ms Wiz, opening her sleeve so that he could return home. "That's really nice news."

"I've had enough," said the producer, getting to his feet. "I'm going to shut that woman up and read the news myself."

"And there's also good news for Paranormal Operatives," Ms Wiz was saying, when the producer walked briskly into the news studio. He was just about to lift Ms Wiz out of her chair when viewers throughout the country heard a faint humming noise. There was a flash of smoke – and there, in the place of the producer, stood a panda, blinking its eyes in the studio lights.

"We've just received a late news flash," said Ms Wiz. "A television producer has been turned into a panda. As everyone knows, the panda is a threatened species. In fact—" Ms Wiz pulled the panda's ear "—I'm threatening this one right now."

The panda slunk miserably out of the studio.

"Can I have a ride?" asked Little Musha, climbing on its broad back as it returned to the control room.

"As I was saying," Ms Wiz smiled at the camera, "the good news for Paranormal Operatives is that the word 'witch' is to be banned from dictionaries. I asked a well-known Paranormal Operative – me – why the ban was necessary. 'Well,' I answered myself, 'the word "witch"

suggests to a lot of people that to be magic you have to be an ugly old woman with cobwebs in your hair. This, of course, isn't true.' 'Why not?' I asked. 'Because,' I replied, 'magic belongs to all ages and to men as well as women, although, between me and me, women are rather better at it.' 'Thank you, Ms Wiz'," said Ms Wiz.

"This is getting very strange," said Caroline.

"Finally news of a really nice record achieved today. Little Musha Smith of 91 Elmtree Road has stayed up after ten o'clock and only burst into tears once. 'We're really proud of her,' said sister Caroline. 'Apart from pulling Jimmy's nose and then stamping on his foot, she has been an angel'."

"Hey, Musha," Caroline called out. "You're on the news."

But Little Musha was too busy riding the panda to pay any attention.

"Typical," sighed Caroline.

CHAPTER FIVE
A LOVELY PERF

For a girl who had spent the evening inside her parents' television set with her favourite Paranormal Operative and a little sister who was now behaving quite well, Caroline was feeling surprisingly sad.

"Heigh-ho," Ms Wiz was saying, as they wandered along yet another corridor. "I really enjoyed that."

"You did seem to be having quite a lot of fun," said Caroline pointedly. "Just like Little Musha had quite a lot of fun earlier. Almost everyone has been having fun."

Ms Wiz smiled. "Anyway," she said, "we'd better head back to the real world. Your mum and dad will be home soon."

"I'm going to tell them about pulling Jimmy's nose," said Little Musha.

"What about my newsreading?" Ms Wiz laughed. "I always wanted to do that. The producer was quite upset about it."

"He'd still be galumphing about as a panda if I hadn't reminded you to turn him back into a producer," said Caroline quietly.

"Yes, thank goodness you were there," said Ms Wiz.

"I'm always there," said Caroline grumpily. "It's just like home in this television set. I keep Musha out of trouble. I even have to sort things out when the great Ms Wiz is having a good time. Why have I always got to be sensible and grown-up? When is it my turn to enjoy myself?"

Ms Wiz gave a little smile as they

walked past a door marked "GREEN ROOM".

"That's where the actors rest," she said. "Hey, you like acting, don't you, Caroline? Would you like to see if there's anyone there?"

Caroline shrugged. "If you like," she said.

Ms Wiz opened the door to reveal a man and a woman in Victorian costume. They both were pacing backwards and forwards and seemed rather upset.

"Wow," whispered Caroline. "It's Nigel Triffroll and Dulcima de Trop, the famous actors."

"What have I *always* said?" Nigel was clasping his brow. "Never agree to act with children or animals."

"And that ghastly little Jane was a bit of both," said Dulcima, fanning herself with a copy of *The Stage*.

"Very droll, darling," said Nigel.

"What appears to be the trouble?" asked Ms Wiz.

The two actors turned to them without showing the least surprise.

"Only that the little brute of a small girl who was supposed to appear in the last episode of *Heritage*, our wonderful costume drama, has got tonsillitis," said Dulcima.

"Tonsillitis, hah!" cried Nigel with a dismissive wave of the arm. "Otherwise known as stage fright."

"Why don't I do it?" asked
Caroline.

Nigel and Dulcima looked at her in
amazement.

"Are you a thesp?" asked Nigel.

"A what?"

Nigel sighed with impatience. "Do
you tread the boards?" he said.

"If you mean, 'Does she act?',"
said Ms Wiz. "The answer is, 'Yes,
brilliantly'."

"Saved!" cried Dulcima. "Here are
your lines." She gave Caroline a
script. "Are you a quick learner?"

Caroline gulped. "Er, quite," she
said nervously.

"The part you play is of a scruffy
little chimney-sweep girl who turns
out to be the Duchess of Portland,"
said Nigel. "Just be yourself,
darling."

"We're on in five minutes," said
Dulcima, grabbing Caroline's hand.

"I'll take you to make-up and we can learn the lines together."

"Why's Caroline all dirty?" asked Little Musha a few minutes later, as she and Ms Wiz watched *Heritage* on a small television in the Green Room.

"Ssshhh!" said Ms Wiz, sitting nervously on the edge of her seat. "I think she's the best chimney-sweep I've ever seen on television."

At that moment, the camera closed in dramatically upon Caroline's face. "You mean," she said, as tears welled up in her eyes. "You mean that I'm your *daughter*?"

"Welcome home," said Dulcima with a dazzling smile.

As Nigel, Dulcima and Caroline embraced, the theme music for *Heritage* swelled up behind them.

"Did Caroline do well?" asked
Little Musha.

"She was astonishing," said Ms
Wiz, dabbing her eyes.

Moments later, the door to the
Green Room was flung open and
the three actors entered.

"A star is born!" announced
Dulcima. "Caroline, you were
wonderful, darling. Wasn't she
wonderful, Nigel?"

"Lovely perf," said Nigel, adding
with a hint of sulkiness, " I didn't
think I was bad either."

"You were wonderful too," said
Caroline.

Ms Wiz looked at a nearby clock.
"Never mind the 'wonderful
darlings'," she said. "If we don't
hurry, your parents will be returning
to an empty house."

"What about my clothes?" asked
Caroline.

"Here they are," said Ms Wiz. "There's no time to take the soot off your face."

Caroline wriggled out of her clothes. "Bye, Nigel and Dulcie," she said breathlessly. "That was definitely the best fun I've ever had."

"Cheery-bye, darling," said Nigel.

Dulcima gave Caroline a kiss. "Will we be able to work together again soon?" she asked.

"I hope so," said Caroline.

Ms Wiz, Caroline and Little Musha ran as fast as they could down a long corridor.

"What about Herbert?" gasped Musha.

"I thought you didn't like rats," said Caroline.

"Poor Herbert! Left alone in television land."

"Don't worry," shouted Ms Wiz. "I've got him."

They ran up the stairs and through a trapdoor at the top.

"Home!" said Little Musha as, once again, they stood on top of the Smiths' television set. Just then, they all heard the sound of a key turning in the front door.

"Quick, Ms Wiz!" said Caroline. "Get us back to our normal size before my parents come in."

There was a humming noise from

the direction of Ms Wiz, and the next
thing Caroline and Little Musha
knew, they had fallen in a heap on the
living-room floor. Everything in the
room appeared to be back to normal.

"Well," said Mrs Smith, looking at
the tangle of bodies on the floor. "Still
up at eleven o'clock? I don't call
that very good babysitting."

"We couldn't sleep," said Caroline.
"I thought that, because tomorrow's

Saturday, it wouldn't matter too much."

"It doesn't," said Mr Smith, putting his arm around his wife's waist. "We've had a good time, so why shouldn't you?"

"Caroline," said Mrs Smith. "Your face is absolutely filthy. What have you been doing?"

Just then, the telephone rang. Mr and Mrs Smith looked at one another in surprise.

"Hullo," said Mrs Smith into the phone. "Yes . . . brilliant, I see. Could you call tomorrow after I've discussed it with her and her father?"

"Who was it?" asked Mr Smith.

"It was a television producer," said Mrs Smith, looking puzzled. "He told me he thought Caroline was so good in something called *Heritage*, he wanted her to act in other programmes."

"Perhaps you ought to tell them

about it, Ms Wiz," smiled Caroline.

"Ms Wiz!" gasped Little Musha. "You're getting *smaller*!"

"Oh no!" said Caroline. "Don't leave me to explain it all."

Ms Wiz winked. "Whenever magic's needed, I'll be back," she said, smiling at Caroline. "Magic – and fun."

"I can't believe my eyes," said Mr Smith.

"She's really tiny now," said Little Musha. There was a little pop, like a bubble bursting, and Ms Wiz had disappeared.

For a moment, the Smith family stood in silence.

"Could you kindly tell us what's been going on?" said Mrs Smith finally.

"It's a long story," said Caroline. "And I think you had better sit down first."

POWER-CRAZY
Ms Wiz

Acknowledgement

I would like to thank the children of Class 12D, Riverside Primary School, Wallasey, whose idea Ms Wiz PM was the inspiration for this story.

CHAPTER ONE
A LEAN, MEAN
PETER HARRIS

It was the first day of the holidays, the fair
was in town and the sun shone high in the
sky. But for Peter Harris, better known as
Podge, it felt like the worst day of his life.

He wandered through the fairground,
thinking of the bad news he had received
that morning. The Big Dipper loomed up
in front of him but he walked on. He heard
the screams and laughter of children on the
Waltza – he hardly looked at them. Even the
candyfloss store, which was normally
Podge's first stop at the fair, didn't interest
him today.

Deep in thought, he found himself
standing in front of a small, circular store
decked out with plastic toys and goldfish
in transparent plastic bags. There was a
table in the middle with some wooden

cubes on it. A sign on the stall read "GET THE HOOP OVER THE CUBE – TAKE A GOLDFISH HOME!"

"Want a go, son?" The stallholder, a red-faced man whose large stomach stretched his dirty white shirt, held out a hoop.

Podge shook his head. He never won anything. Anyway, he wasn't in the mood.

He was just about to move away when

he noticed that one of the fishes seemed to
be looking at him with that wide-eyed
help-me expression that Podge's friend
Henry Wilson put on when there was a
maths test at school. Podge frowned – he
didn't want to think of school right now.

"Yes, we'll have a go, please."

Podge turned to see, standing beside
him, a girl in torn jeans and a baseball cap.
The stallholder gave her a hoop which she
passed to Podge.

"No, thanks," said Podge quietly. "I'm useless at throwing things."

"Not today you aren't," said the girl.

Sighing, Podge held the hoop before him and took aim. As he drew his hand back, he was aware of a humming sound all around him. Now where had he heard that before? Concentrating as hard as he could, he let the hoop go.

It moved through the air slowly, like a tiny spacecraft, and hovered over the block, before settling neatly around it.

"Eh?" The stallholder looked at the hoop suspiciously.

"Brilliant throw!" said the girl. "We'll have this goldfish, please." She pointed to the fish which Podge had noticed.

Podge looked at her more closely. She was a bit older than he had thought at first and there was something familiar about her flashing green eyes. "Haven't we met somewhere?" Podge asked.

Without a word, she held up her hand.

On her nails was black nail-varnish.

"Ms Wiz!" Podge smiled for the first time that day. "What are you doing here?"

"You know how it is," said Ms Wiz quietly. "I go wherever magic is needed."

Grumpily, the stallholder handed her the goldfish. "Magic," he muttered. "Looked like good old-fashioned cheating to me."

Ms Wiz put her arm around Podge's shoulders. "So," she said. "Tell me your problem."

"I thought you knew everything," said Podge, turning away from the stall. Ms Wiz followed, holding the goldfish in front of her.

"Not everything," she said. "The message I received this morning was 'MAGIC ALERT – PODGE HARRIS – PARENT PROBLEM'."

"*Major* parent problem," said Podge gloomily. "I'm not sure I really want to talk about it."

Ms Wiz walked into a video arcade

and stood in front of a computer game. "When did the problem take place?" she asked.

"This morning at breakfast."

"And your address is . . . ?"

"15 Rylett Road."

Ms Wiz pressed a few buttons on the machine. Briefly the screen went fuzzy and made a quiet humming sound. Then it cleared to show a modern kitchen. In the centre of the room was a table on either side of which sat a man and a woman, looking very serious. Between them was a child, eating.

"Hey, that's me!" Podge gasped. "That's my kitchen! And there's Mum and Dad!"

"It's a magical reconstruction of your kitchen at breakfast this morning. It's going to show me what happened."

"Oh no." Podge winced. "This is going to be really embarrassing."

*

On the screen, the figures started talking.

"Now Peter, we need to have a serious discussion," Podge's father, Mr Harris, was saying.

"Voff avout?" said Podge.

"*Don't* talk with your mouth full," Mr Harris snapped.

"Podge swallowed. "Sorry," he said.

"Today's the start of your holidays, Peter," his father continued. "And from now on there are going to be some changes around here."

"Changes?"

"Number one, you're going to spend less time with your nose in a book, reading stories, and more time learning for exams."

"But—"

"Number two, you're going on a diet. You look like a football on legs. So it's no more chocolate biscuits. This time next month I want to see a lean, mean Peter Harris."

"Lean? Mean?"

"Number three." Mr Harris paused. "I'm taking you away from that school of yours."

Podge gasped.

"St Barnabas." Mr Harris spat the words out in disgust. "All you get there is . . . larking about."

"What about my friends?" Podge protested.

"There'll be time enough for friends when you've passed a few exams," said Mr Harris, getting to his feet. "My decision's final and I won't budge. Will I, Mother?"

"No," Mrs Harris had sighed wearily. "You won't budge."

"Hmm, I see the problem now," said Ms Wiz, as the images faded from the screen. "Somehow we've got to make your father change his mind."

"Some hope," Podge muttered. "You'd

have to be Prime Minister to make my dad change his mind."

"Hey, great vid!" said a voice behind them. Ms Wiz and Podge turned to see Jack Beddows, Podge's best friend. "What did you have to do to win?" said Jack, looking at the screen. "Get the big boy through the kitchen door?"

"Great joke," said Podge.

"I saw you with Ms Wiz," said Jack. "I thought you were playing a game."

"That was no game," said Ms Wiz. "It was real – Podge is being taken away from St Barnabas. It's time for action." She walked out of the video arcade in the direction of the dodgem cars.

"I don't believe it," Jack said to Podge.

"And I'm being put on a diet," said Podge. "My dad says I look like a football on legs. That's not true, is it?"

"Er, well—"

Fortunately for Jack, they were interrupted by Ms Wiz waving to them from a purple dodgem car. "Come on," she shouted. "We've got no time to lose."

"Typical Ms Wiz," said Podge. "It's the most serious day of my life and she wants to ride a bumper car."

Both of them squeezed into the dodgem, with Podge in the driving seat.

"I say." A man eating some candy floss nearby pointed to the dodgem car. "You're only allowed two people per car, you know. I think one of you really ought to get out."

"Do you?" said Ms Wiz innocently.

As the man walked towards a fairground assistant, the candyfloss he was holding seemed to be growing larger and larger until, seconds later, it covered the whole of his head and the top of his body.

"Help!" he shouted in a muffled voice.

"Where am I? Everything's gone pink."

"Let's go," said Ms Wiz. She reached under her seat and took out a white umbrella which she fixed to the front of the dodgem. It began to turn, faster and faster, like the propeller of a helicopter.

"Er, no, Ms Wiz," said Podge nervously as the dodgem floated upwards. "I don't think this is one of your better ideas."

But the dodgem seemed to have a life of its own. It climbed higher and higher over the fairground.

"Brilliant ride," said Jack. "And we didn't even pay."

"I hate heights!" Podge was clinging on to the steering wheel. "I get travel-sick. This is meant to be a bumper car, not a bumper plane."

As the dodgem picked up speed, Ms Wiz took off her baseball cap and let the wind blow through her long, dark hair. "London, here we come."

"Why are we going to London?" Jack asked.

"Didn't I tell you?" Ms Wiz raised her voice above the whistling of the wind.

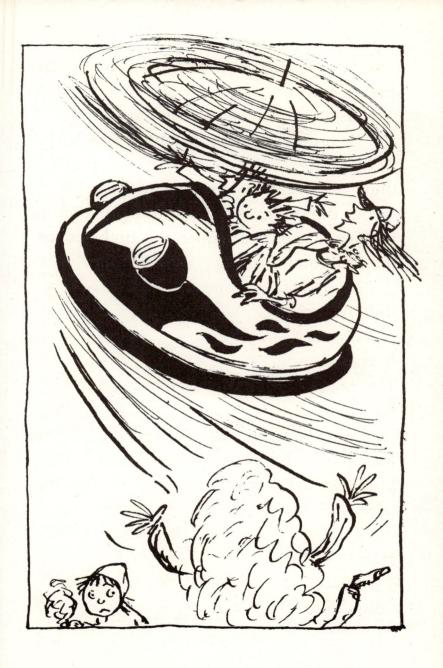

"We're off to see the Prime Minister. It was Podge's idea."

"*What?*" said Podge. "I never—"

"Well done, Podge," shouted Jack.

CHAPTER TWO
MAD GOLDFISH DISEASE

A purple dodgem car, suspended by a whirling white umbrella, flew high over the streets of London.

As it skimmed a few feet above Buckingham Palace, it seemed to be slowing down.

"Now here's what we're going to do," said Ms Wiz to Podge and Jack. "In a few moments' time, we shall be meeting the Prime Minister—"

"Yeah yeah," muttered Jack who didn't believe anything until he could see it.

"—and I shall be asking him to pass a new law to prevent parents taking children away from schools against their wishes."

"Are you sure he can pass laws all by himself?" asked Podge.

"Of course he can," said Ms Wiz. "He's Prime Minister, isn't he?"

"I think it may be a bit more complicated than that," said Jack.

"Honestly, you two!" Ms Wiz crossed her arms, almost crushing the goldfish she was carrying. "You're so . . . negative. Just trust me."

"We'll have to," said Jack, looking over the edge of the dodgem. "We're coming in to land."

"Now it's very important that we act as a team," said Ms Wiz. "I'll be in charge, Podge will be my adviser and Jack will look after Henry?"

"Henry?"

"Named after Henry Wilson at school," said Podge.

Ms Wiz passed Jack the bag containing the goldfish. "This is Henry," she smiled. "He's very important."

"Typical," grumbled Jack. "Ms Wiz gets the power, Podge gets the fun and I get the goldfish."

The dodgem hovered a few feet above a wide pavement. As it landed, a small crowd of people gathered on the pavement, staring and pointing.

A tall, bearded policeman pushed his way towards them. Taking one look at the dodgem, he reached into his top pocket for a notebook. "No number plates," he muttered to himself. "Parked in a bus lane. Driver under age."

Ms Wiz stepped out of the dodgem and Podge noticed that, while they had been travelling, her clothes had changed from a torn T-shirt to a smart grey suit. "I'm sorry about our parking, officer," she said. "We had to stop here because we're looking for an animal hospital."

"Oh yeah?" The policeman drew himself up to his full height. "I don't see no animals."

Without a word, Ms Wiz took the bag containing Henry the goldfish from Jack.

"Look at him, the poor little creature." She held the bag in front of the policeman's face. "He's suffering from Mad Goldfish Disease. Swimming round and round – going bonkers before your very eyes."

"Don't be daft, lady," said the policeman, his eyes following Henry. "All goldfish do that."

"But they don't do this," said Ms Wiz

under her breath, as a distant humming
noise could be heard. "You are now feeling
very . . . drowsy," she said. "You want . . .
to . . . go . . . to . . . sleep."

"I don't believe it," whispered Jack.
"She's using Henry to hypnotise the
policeman."

Slowly Ms Wiz lowered the bag. The
policeman continued to stare into space, his
mouth hanging open.

"You are now under my spell," said Ms

Wiz quietly. "You will do everything you are told. Do you understand?"

"Yes, ma'am," said the policeman.

"Please take me to the Prime Minister's house."

"Yes, ma'am."

"Then come back and make sure no one touches our dodgem."

"No, ma'am. I mean, yes, ma'am."

The policeman turned and slowly, like a sleepwalker, made his way past a barrier and into a quiet side road.

"It's Downing Street," whispered Podge, who had seen a street sign. "This is where the Prime Minister lives."

The policeman reached Number Ten, Downing Street and knocked on the door. "Who shall I say is calling, Ma'am?" he asked.

"Ms Wisdom, Mr Peter Harris and Mr Jack Beddows," said Ms Wiz.

A young woman with neat blonde hair and a neat blue suit opened the door.

"Ms Beddows, Mr Jack Peters and Mr Wisdom Harris to see the Prime Minister," said the policeman in a distant voice.

"Great memory," Jack muttered.

"I'm afraid the Prime Minister is too busy to see anyone but—"

"Too busy?" Ms Wiz pushed forward. "This is important. What's he doing?"

"He's just . . . busy," said the woman, her smile becoming less friendly. "The country doesn't just run itself, you know. Now, my name's Marjorie and I'm from the Prime Minister's office – I'm sure I can help you."

"I don't think so," said Ms Wiz. "This is a highly confidential matter."

"Then in that case, I suggest you write a letter and . . . and . . ." As a faint hum could be heard, Marjorie stopped speaking and stood as motionlessly as if she had been frozen.

"Sorry, Marje," said Ms Wiz, stepping past her into the house. "I'll just have to put a statue spell on you for the moment."

Jack looked nervously at Podge. "I've never seen her this determined," he muttered, as they followed her into the house.

"Now," said Ms Wiz, looking around the dark hall of Number Ten, Downing Street, "I wonder where the person in charge is."

"Why, that must be me."

A man in a dark suit stood at the foot of the stairs in front of them. "Would you mind telling me what you're doing in my house?" he said.

Podge gulped. "It's the P-P-Prime—"

"He looks smaller than he does on telly," said Jack.

Ms Wiz smiled politely. "Marjorie told us you were too busy to see us."

"She was right," said the Prime Minister.

"And we have a problem," said Ms Wiz, extending her hand backwards towards Jack. "He's called Henry."

"Henry?"

"Yes." Ms Wiz held the plastic bag before

the Prime Minister's eyes. "Just look at him." Henry swam round and round and round . . . "You want to go . . . to . . . sleep."

"Why—" The Prime Minister swayed slightly as he spoke in a distant voice. "Why it's a . . . goldfish."

"Prime Minister," said Ms Wiz. "You are now in my power."

CHAPTER THREE
ORDER! ORDER!

At 15 Rylett Road, Podge's father Cuthbert
Harris was crouched over a pile of wood
with a screwdriver in his hand.

"This new desk I've bought will be a
surprise for the lad," he was saying to Mrs
Harris, who watched him as he tried to
make sense of the instructions. "It shows
that we're doing our bit. He works harder,
loses his story books, goes on a diet, gives
up chocolate biscuits, says goodbye to his
friends and leaves his school, we buy him
a desk. That's fair, isn't it?" He frowned.
"Now I wonder how this leg goes."

Without a word, Mrs Harris took the
screwdriver from her husband and began
to assemble the desk.

"Action, that's the thing," said Mr
Harris, leaning against the wall. "In this

life, there are doers and watchers. I want our lad to do things – like his father."

"Pass me that screw, will you, Cuthbert," said Mrs Harris, who was already on the second leg of the desk.

"The lad's got to learn. It's dog-eat-dog out there."

"Talking of learning—" Mrs Harris reached for the third leg "—why have you taken Peter's books from his shelves?"

"I'm chucking them out," said Mr

Harris. "They're just stories. Those bookshelves will be needed for the exam guides I've bought." He reached inside a plastic bag beside him. "There's *Mathematics for Exams, Geography for Exams, English for Exams*." He opened one of the books.

Mrs Harris picked up the fourth leg of the desk.

"Listen to this, Mother." Mr Harris stabbed a fat finger at the book in his hand.

"It says here, 'Welcome to *English for Exams*. This little guide will help you pass your English tests. The most important thing to remember is that the more books you read, the better you'll be at English.' " Mr Harris frowned, then continued, " 'It doesn't matter what books you read so long as you enjoy . . .' " His voice trailed off.

"Interesting." Mrs Harris smiled to herself as she screwed in the desk's last leg.

"Oh, all right." Podge's father shrugged impatiently. "I suppose Peter can keep his books if he likes."

Mrs Harris stood up and looked at her work with satisfaction. "I wonder where he's got to?" she said.

At that moment, Podge was sitting between Ms Wiz and Jack at a long, shiny table in the Cabinet Room at Number Ten, Downing Street. Facing them was the Prime Minister.

"So that's our problem, Prime

Minister," Ms Wiz was saying. "All we
need you to do is pass a law that will
prevent Mr Harris taking Podge away from
St Barnabas."

The Prime Minister smiled. "I'm glad you
raised that point," he said. "But, at the
end of the day, we're not playing on a level
playing-field. Someone has moved the goal-
posts. We're in a whole different ballgame."

"I beg your pardon?" Ms Wiz looked confused.

"Don't panic, Ms Wiz," said Jack quietly. "This is just the way politicians talk. You have to ask the question again."

"Can you please help us, Prime Minister?"

"That's a very good question," said the Prime Minister. "But, as I've said on a number of occasions, there's a whole range of options and—"

Ms Wiz banged the table. "Yes or no, PM?"

"Er . . . no."

"Why not?" Podge asked. "You're meant to be the person in charge."

"Parliament," said the Prime Minister. "Laws have to go through Parliament."

For a moment there was silence in the Cabinet Room. "That's it then," said Podge eventually. "Not even Ms Wiz could hynotise the whole of Parliament."

"Unless . . ." An odd smile had appeared on the Prime Minister's face. "Unless someone came with me to the Houses of

Parliament this afternoon. Someone who could make a speech."

"Ms Wiz," said Podge.

"No no," said Ms Wiz. "I couldn't possibly. I don't think magic and politics mix."

"Come on," said Jack. "You've taught Class Five. It would be a piece of cake after that."

"Do it for me," begged Podge.

"I think you'd do it very well," said the Prime Minister. "I'll introduce you to the House of Commons and Marjorie can look after Podge and Jack, if you'll just let her move around again."

Ms Wiz sighed. "Oh, all right," she said. "Just a *little* speech."

"Yeah!" said Jack. "Vote for Ms Wiz!"

"Order, order!"

Thirty minutes later, Podge and Jack were looking down on the House of

Commons from a high balcony where they had been taken by Marjorie.

"The government MPs are on one side and the opposition MPs are on the other," Marjorie whispered. "The person in the wig, who keeps saying 'Order, order', is called the Speaker. She's meant to keep everyone under control."

"She's not doing much of a job," muttered Jack. "I've seen more order in the last Assembly of term at St Barnabas."

"But where's the Prime Minister? Where's Ms Wiz?" asked Podge.

As he spoke, an odd growling sound came from the MPs below them. They seemed to be looking towards the door.

"Here they come," said Marjorie.

Slowly the Prime Minister made his way between the rows of MPs. Pale but dignified, Ms Wiz followed him. As they took their seats on the front bench, the Speaker pointed towards them.

"Pray silence for the Prime Minister," she said loudly.

The Prime Minister stood up. "Er, actually," he said, "I'm not going to make a speech this afternoon—"

"Good!" shouted one of the MPs opposite.

"Run out of words, have you?" laughed another.

"How rude," said Podge. "I hope they're not this mean to Ms Wiz."

"Instead, I've asked my good friend Ms Wiz to speak on my behalf."

An astonished silence descended on the chamber.

Ms Wiz rose to her feet. "Thanks, PM," she said. "Now, the reason why I've decided to talk to you this afternoon is that I want you to pass a law to help a boy called Peter Harris."

"Order, order," the Speaker interrupted. "What on earth is going on here? You can't just wander in here and announce that you want to make a law—"

A faint humming sound filled the House of Commons.

"Hoo hoo hoo."

The children stared at the Speaker in amazement. In her place, there now sat a small grey monkey jumping up and down angrily.

One of the MPs on the front bench facing Ms Wiz stood up. "I must object to a complete stranger coming into the House and somehow replacing Madam Speaker with a monkey. This is absolutely . . . whaaaahhhahhhaahhh."

In his place stood a gorilla, thumping his chest.

"Uh-oh," said Jack. "Something tells me Ms Wiz is losing control of this situation."

"Now Peter Harris likes his—" Ms Wiz raised her voice above the noise of interruptions "—he likes his food—". Every MP who stood up to say something was turned into a different kind of monkey.

Soon her words were being drowned by

the noise of chattering, angry, scratching monkeys.

Ms Wiz looked about her and frowned. "We shall return," she said, pulling the Prime Minister to his feet and backing towards the door. "We shall work on our speech at Number Ten, Downing Street."

"I suppose that's it then," said Jack, getting to his feet. "We'd better go home."

Podge followed gloomily. "Ms Wiz was right about one thing," he said. "Politics and magic don't mix."

CHAPTER FOUR
A MESSAGE FROM THE PM

The Prime Minister's car moved slowly through the crowds that had gathered outside the Houses of Parliament.

On the back seat Podge and Jack sat between the Prime Minister and Marjorie. Ms Wiz was in the front, waving to the crowd.

"What's happened to Ms Wiz?" Jack whispered to Podge. "One speech to the House of Commons and suddenly she's behaving like she's the Queen or something."

"And it wasn't exactly the greatest speech ever made," grumbled Podge. "We'll never get my dad to change his mind now."

"Cameras, television, that's what you want," said the Prime Minister in a strange, dreamlike voice.

"Oh, Prime Minister—" Ms Wiz smiled modestly. "All this fame – and so soon."

"I meant for Podge," said the Prime Minister. "If we want his parents to change their mind, we'll need publicity. Television."

"That's it!" Jack turned to Podge. "If you appeared on television, your dad would *have* to pay attention. You'd be the week's good cause – Podge-Aid."

"Marjorie, I want to speak to the nation with Ms Wiz," said the Prime Minister suddenly. "In half an hour's time."

"B-but, sir." Marjorie had turned pale. "We're only meant to do that when there's a national emergency."

"This is an emergency. Podge is being forced to leave St Barnabas."

"Anyway," said Marjorie, "it's a terrible time to appear on television – everyone will be waiting to watch that daily soap opera, *The Avenue.*"

"Dad's favourite programme!" said Podge.

"Perfect." The Prime Minister smiled. "Get the cameras round as soon as we arrive."

"My speech!" In the front seat, Ms Wiz stopped waving for a moment. "I must work on my speech."

"Crazy," sighed Jack.

Mr Harris was exhausted. He had helped Mrs Harris while she was assembling the desk. He had watched while she tidied all the books in the bedroom. He had stood by, offering advice while Mrs Harris worked out a diet that would help produce a lean, mean Peter Harris.

"Phew," he said, flopping into an armchair in front of the television. "Any chance of a cup of tea, Mother?"

"No, Cuthbert." Mrs Harris sat down beside him. "I made the desk. You make

the tea. There's just time before *The Avenue*."

Grumbling, Mr Harris stood up. "Work, work, work," he muttered.

"I can't think where Peter's got to," said Mrs Harris. "He was meant to be back an hour ago."

"Having too much fun probably," Mr Harris called out from the kitchen. "There'll be an end to that with the new school."

Grumbling, he returned to the sitting room and switched on the television.

"There's now a change to the advertised programme," said the TV announcer. "Instead of *The Avenue*, we'll be going over live in a few moments to Number Ten, Downing Street for a message from the Prime Minister."

"Oh *no!*" said Mr Harris.

The Prime Minister's office was lit up by television lights.

A rather large television producer, called Miss Barkworth, was fussing around with the papers on the Prime Minister's desk. "This is all most irregular, sir," she said. "We haven't even been given a script for you to read from the autocue."

"What's an autocue?" Jack asked Podge as they watched the preparations.

"It's the little screen they read from

when they're making a speech on telly,"
Podge whispered.

"I don't need a script," the Prime
Minister was telling the producer. "My
colleague Ms Wiz will be doing most of the
talking."

"But who is this Wiz person?" The
producer lowered her voice as she saw Ms
Wiz pacing nervously backwards and
forwards in the office. "Has she ever done
any public speaking?"

"She spoke to the House of Commons
this afternoon," said the Prime Minister.
"An excellent speech, it was."

"Yeah," muttered Jack. "She made
monkeys of them."

Ms Wiz stood in front of the mirror,
rehearsing her lines. "Ladies and
gentlemen," she said, then frowned. "No,
too serious . . . Hullo, everybody! No,
that's wrong . . . Hi, my name's Ms Wiz—"

"Just be yourself," smiled Podge. "You'll
be fine."

"Thirty seconds before we're on air," shouted Miss Barkworth, scurrying behind the camera. "I want the PM at his desk, Ms Wiz standing beside him and the fat boy a bit to the left."

"She's not exactly Miss Skinny herself," murmured Jack as he moved out of camera range.

"Sshh!" The producer held up five fingers, then four ... three ... two ... one ...

The Prime Minister switched on his most sincere smile as a red light appeared above the camera.

"Hullo," he said. "I expect you're all wondering why I decided to speak to the nation this afternoon ..."

CHAPTER FIVE
A LADY NOT FOR TURNING

Mr Harris sat grumpily in front of the television set, a mug of tea in his hand.

"Politicians!" he said to Mrs Harris. "You work hard, you do your best for your lad. All you ask in return is the chance to relax in front of *The Avenue*. But no—"

"It must be something really important," said Mrs Harris. "People don't interrupt *The Avenue* for nothing."

"Publicity, Mother." Mr Harris slurped his tea. "Your average politician will do anything for publicity."

"And so," the Prime Minister was saying on television, "I would now like to hand you over to my friend and colleague, Ms Wiz."

"Ms Wiz?" Mr Harris sat forward in his chair. "Isn't that the woman who turned up at St Barnabas and sent a rat up the school inspector's trousers?"

"What on earth is she doing there?" asked Mrs Harris.

"I always knew that woman spelt trouble—"

"Shush, Cuthbert," said Mrs Harris. "Let's hear what she has to say."

Ms Wiz sat easily on the edge of the Prime Minister's desk. "This afternoon I want to tell you the story of a little boy," she said. "Just an ordinary lad. He likes his books. He likes his friends. He likes his chocolate biscuits."

As she smiled, the camera moved closer to her face.

"Yet this little boy's father has decided to drag him away from his school, his lovely childhood friends—"

"Poor little mite," said Mr Harris.

"—his nice stories—"

"What a shame," said Mr Harris.

"—even his chocolate biscuits."

Mr Harris shook his head. "Some parents don't deserve to have children," he said.

"Is this fair?" The woman on the television glanced to her right. "Look at this boy. Is he really so fat?"

She paused as the camera turned to show a child in the shadows of the office.

"Yes, all right, perhaps he is a bit . . . plump," Ms Wiz smiled. "But maybe he eats food as a way of expressing himself, as a way of asking for love from his mum and dad. Maybe every chocolate biscuit that

he eats is not so much a chocolate biscuit as a cry for help—"

"And the little thing looks just like our Peter," sobbed Mrs Harris.

"I don't care who he is." Mr Harris blew his nose on a big red handkerchief. "That boy's parents should be more understanding."

"So I ask you all today," the woman continued, "listen to your children. They have the right to have friends, books – even chocolate biscuits now and then. Let the

example of Podge Harris be an example to us all."

Mr and Mrs Harris stopped crying and stared at one another in amazement.

"Podge Harris?" they said.

The cameras had left Number Ten, Downing Street but Ms Wiz was behaving more and more strangely.

"Where are my ministers?" she asked, looking about her as she sat at the Prime Minister's desk. "I want to go to Parliament and make some laws."

"You did brilliantly, Ms Wiz," said Podge. "But I think we ought to be on our way home. Our parents will be getting worried."

"Home?" Ms Wiz looked shocked. "But my work here has just begun. This lady is not for turning."

"I'm starving," muttered Podge.

"Now, PM—" Ms Wiz beckoned to the

back of the room where the Prime Minister stood with Marjorie and Miss Barkworth. "I'd like to discuss some new laws that we'll be making."

"But Ms Wiz—" The Prime Minister smiled politely. "You've turned most of Parliament into monkeys."

"The spell will have worn off by now," said Ms Wiz. "But I could do it again if you like. Yes, that's a good idea. If people disagree with us, I'll just change them into monkeys."

"What are we going to do with her?" Podge whispered to Jack. "She's gone power-crazy."

Jack was staring at Henry the goldfish, whose plastic bag he had put on a bookshelf nearby. "What we need is a bit of magic to help us. A bit of Henry magic." He picked up the bag. "Oh no, Ms Wiz," he said loudly. "Look what's happened."

Frowning, Ms Wiz turned. "What's the problem, Jack?" she asked.

"It's Henry. He's been dazzled by the television lights." He held the fish up in front of Ms Wiz's eyes. "Ms Wiz," he said, "You want to go . . . to . . . sleep."

Ms Wiz stared straight ahead of her.

Podge gulped. "I don't believe it!" he gasped. "You've hypnotised Ms Wiz."

"She said Henry had his own magic. I thought it might work on her and it did." Jack smiled. "Ms Wiz, you are now going to say goodbye to the Prime Minister," he said.

"Goodbye, Prime Minister," said Ms Wiz in a sleepy voice.

"Goodbye, Ms Wiz," said the Prime Minister.

"You will ask him to pass a law banning all schools."

"Jack!" Podge grabbed his arm. "Don't mess about – let's go home."

"That was a joke, Ms Wiz," said Jack quickly. "Please take us back to the purple dodgem and then fly us home."

"Anything you say, Jack," said Ms Wiz.

They walked slowly towards the front door. "Shouldn't you take the spell off the Prime Minister?" Marjorie asked. "Otherwise he'll be staring into space and talking like a computer for ever."

Jack looked at the Prime Minister for a moment. "I don't think anyone will notice the difference," he said.

"Thanks, PM," Podge shouted back.

"Good luck, Podge," said the Prime Minister, closing the door of Number Ten, Downing Street behind them.

The purple dodgem hovered just above 15 Rylett Road before landing gently on the Harrises' carefully tended lawn.

"Peter!" Mrs Harris opened the front door. "We were so worried about you."

Mr Harris appeared behind his wife. "We saw you on telly, son. You looked great."

"Dad's been thinking," said Mrs Harris, nudging her husband.

"Have I?" Mr Harris frowned. "Oh yes."
He placed his arm around Podge's
shoulder. "Son," he said, "maybe I was a
bit . . . hasty this morning."

"You mean about the books and the
biscuits and St Barnabas?" asked Podge.

"That's right." Mr Harris managed a
smile.

"Yeah," said Jack. "Good old Mr Harris!
And it's all thanks to Ms Wiz."

They turned to the purple dodgem

where Ms Wiz was still sitting motionlessly.

"What's the matter with her, Jack?" asked Mrs Harris.

"I think she's just feeling a bit tired," said Jack, walking over to the dodgem. He clicked his fingers in front of Ms Wiz's eyes.

"Wha – what?" Ms Wiz shook her head and rubbed her eyes, as if she were just waking up. "I had this weird dream that I went crazy for power."

"Unbelievable," said Jack.

"And—" Ms Wiz started laughing, "I even thought Podge was being taken away from St Barnabas and put on a diet."

"Ridiculous," said Mr Harris.

"Oh well, so long as it was just a dream," said Ms Wiz. "I'd better get this back to the fair." There was a faint humming noise as she drove the purple dodgem back to the road. "I think I'll go by road to the fairground," she said. "The traffic isn't too bad."

"Drive carefully, Ms Wiz," said Podge. "And thank you."

"Bye, Podge. Bye, Jack," she called out. "Bye, Mr and Mrs Harris."

With a roar of the engine, she accelerated away and within seconds had turned the corner of the street and disappeared. For a moment, Mr and Mrs Harris and the children listened as the scream of tyres faded in the distance.

"She may be magic but she's no driver," muttered Mr Harris.

Podge turned into the house. "I'm starving," he said.

"Oh, Peter," said Mrs Harris.

"What about that diet then, son?" Mr Harris asked.

"Podge." Jack stepped forward, holding Henry the goldfish in front of him. "Watch the fishy, please."

Podge hesitated, then followed Henry with his eyes as he swam round and round.

"Can you hear me?" said Jack.

"Yeees." Podge's voice was strange and lifeless. "I can hear you, O master."

"Say after me – I want to go . . . to . . . sleep."

"I want . . . I want . . . I want . . . I want a chocolate biscuit."

Jack shrugged at Mr and Mrs Harris as Podge made for the kitchen.

"Sometimes the magic takes a little time to work," he said.